DISNEY · PIXAR

Merida

The Secret Spell

To Anika —S.B.Q.

randomhousekids.com

ISBN 978-0-7364-3616-8 (hc) — ISBN 978-0-7364-8212-7 (lib. bdg.)

Printed in the United States of America

10 9 8 7 6 5 4 3 2 1

DISNEY · PIXAR

Merida

The Secret Spell

By Sudipta Bardhan-Quallen
Illustrated by Gurihiru

Random House 🏠 New York

Chapter 1

"Good morning, Maudie!"

Merida's voice rang out through the kitchen. Maudie, startled, jiggled the tray of sweet cakes she was holding. It was about to fall over when Merida swooped in and deftly caught it.

"Be careful!" Merida said. "We need all of those for the banquet!"

Maudie sighed with relief as Merida steadied the tray. But her face quickly went from relief to a scowl when Merida plopped a sweet cake in her mouth.

"Princess!" Maudie scolded. "You just agreed we need those!"

Merida shrugged and grinned through a mouthful of cake. "One fewer won't hurt," she mumbled.

Before Maudie could sigh again, Merida quickly kissed her on the cheek and waved good-bye. "Keep up the good work!" she called as she made her way to find Mum.

The halls of Castle DunBroch were empty as Merida wandered up to her parents' room. As she got closer, King Fergus's snores got louder and louder. Merida smiled. *He's not called the Bear King for nothing!*

Merida tiptoed into the bedchamber and gently shook Mum's shoulder.

"What?" Elinor murmured sleepily. "Who's there?"

"Mum!" Merida whispered. "Wake up!"

Elinor blinked. "Merida?" she mumbled as she rubbed her eyes. "It isn't even sunrise. Why are you waking me?"

Merida smiled as Elinor sat up. "I know it's early," she said, "but surely you don't mind a wake-up call from your favorite daughter?"

"You're her only daughter," Fergus grumbled, pulling the blanket over his head.

Merida giggled. "Sorry, Dad."

Elinor leaned over the lump under the blanket and placed a kiss where Fergus's cheek would be. "Go back to sleep, dear."

Fergus grunted.

Mum ushered Merida into the hallway. "Now, what is so urgent, lass? You're never up this early!"

"I need your help to make sure I haven't forgotten anything for the Cardonagh visit!" Merida said. "Preparations for the banquet, decorations for the reception . . ."

"The archery challenge in the highlands?" Elinor added, raising an eyebrow.

Merida blushed. "You know about that?"

"I'm the queen," Elinor replied. "I hear about everything that happens in this kingdom . . . eventually."

"I not only worked on the archery challenge," Merida explained, "I made sure the games field was set for the competitions. Logs for the caber tossing, extra pitchforks for the sheaf toss . . ."

"We wouldn't want to run out of pitchforks again," the queen mumbled.

Merida continued, barely taking a breath. "There's a pile of stones for the stone throw, and space cleared for dancing. I planned the banquet menu with Maudie. We're having kippers and stovies and haggis, of course." Merida and her brothers always found it funny how much their mother enjoyed haggis. "For dessert," Merida went on, "there's cranachan and sweet cakes and scones and—"

"All right, Daughter," Elinor interrupted. "I'm impressed. You've done so much to prepare for today. And I didn't even have to remind you!"

"I want every little thing to be perfect

when Cat gets here," Merida said.

The last time Catriona of Cardonagh came to DunBroch, Merida had been nowhere near this helpful. But that was before she and Cat faced danger, battled Padraic, and forged their friendship. When Cat wrote that she would be visiting again, Merida was thrilled. She'd been counting the hours ever since.

"It seems that the Princess of DunBroch has thought of everything," Elinor said. "I'm very proud of you. Is there anything you need me to do?"

"I suppose not," Merida said, wrapping her arms around Elinor's neck. "I have to get back to work!"

"Good," Elinor answered. "I want to sleep!"

It took most of the morning, but when Merida was done, everything was perfect. And just in time, too—the moment she stepped back to admire her work, a rider appeared on the road to DunBroch, holding up the banner of Cardonagh, the signal that ships were within sight. Cat was nearly here!

In her excitement, Merida almost knocked over the centerpiece she'd just carefully placed on the banquet table. "Ach!" she grunted, lunging to grab it before it fell to the floor. But she was too far away to reach it.

Luckily, Fergus wasn't. "Crivens!" he cried. "What's the hurry, lass?"

"Dad!" Merida said. "Thank you for saving

that!" She took the centerpiece out of Fergus's hands and placed it back where it belonged.

"If you're all done here, would you race me to the docks?" Fergus asked. "My horse needs exercise."

Merida squealed. "Anytime, Dad! Let's go!"

Fergus and Merida were on horseback in an instant. The rest of the DunBroch welcome party watched father and daughter ride off.

"Fergus! Merida!" Elinor shouted. "You're supposed to be part of the official royal welcome! Wait for us!"

"Oh, your mum's calling you," Fergus called out as they raced neck and neck.

"Don't use Mum as your excuse for losing, Dad!" Merida said, spurring Angus on to take the lead.

"Clan DunBroch does not make excuses!"
Fergus roared.

The wind whipped through Merida's hair as
she and Angus sprinted off. Merida won the
race. But the victory hardly mattered when she
spied the Cardonagh ship at the dock. "Do you
see her, Angus?" Merida asked, gazing out to
sea. "Where is Cat?"

Angus whinnied. He couldn't see Cat, either.

Merida heard hoofbeats behind her. Fergus
had finally caught up.

"You beat me, lass," he panted.

But Merida was too distracted to gloat. "I'm trying to find Cat," she said.

"Everyone's coming ashore," Fergus said. "She'll be here soon."

By then, Elinor had maneuvered her horse next to Merida and Angus. "The two of you are very lucky you arrived before the ship," she said. "And you didn't get lost like the last time you raced." She gave her husband and daughter a stern look.

Merida didn't think Mum would be so upset. She and Dad did things like this all the time. But then Elinor smiled, and Merida knew she was only teasing.

Merida and her parents dismounted from their horses and stood calmly at the dock. But

when she spied Cat on the gangplank, Merida's royal manners were forgotten. She waved frantically, trying to get Cat's attention.

But Cat was walking arm in arm with another girl with long golden hair. The two of them were chatting away, not paying attention to anyone else. Merida didn't know who the girl was.

When she reached the shore, Cat finally saw Merida. "Merida!" she squealed, running over to her. "I missed you so much!" She grabbed the other girl's hand and drew her closer. "There's someone I want you to meet. This is Orla, my new cousin. We do everything together!"

"It's like we've been best friends forever!" Orla added.

Best friend? Merida's face clouded over. *I thought that was me.*

Chapter 2

"I missed you, too," Merida said, hugging Cat. To Orla she said, "Welcome to DunBroch."

A trumpet sounded. All eyes turned to the person descending the gangplank. But it wasn't Cat's uncle, Lord Braden. Instead, it was a beautiful woman who looked a lot like Orla.

"That's my new aunt, Fiona," Cat whispered.

"She and Uncle Braden married a few months ago." She gestured toward Orla. "She's Orla's mother. That's how we became cousins."

"Is your uncle here, too?" Merida asked.

Cat shook her head. "No. Aunt Fiona came in his place."

Elinor and Fergus stepped forward to formally greet Fiona. "Welcome, Lady Fiona," Elinor said. Fergus bowed gallantly before their guest.

"Thank you, Queen Elinor," Fiona replied. "My husband sends his regards and regrets that he could not travel with us. As you know, our lands have been ravaged by war. It's only recently that we've been able to bring some peace to our home. Braden felt he couldn't leave Cardonagh now, so he sent me." She smiled. "My husband

spoke often of the deep friendship he forged with you and King Fergus. He hopes, as do I, that the friendship will remain strong and can be extended to me as well."

"We appreciate Braden's continued friendship," Elinor said, "and we look forward to hosting you and getting to know you as well, Lady Fiona. At DunBroch, we believe that the bonds of friendship should stand the test of time."

"And that our clan can never have enough friends!" Fergus added.

A cheer went through the crowd. Cat squeezed Merida's hand.

Merida knew Mum and Dad were right about never having enough friends. She glanced at Orla, who was clapping for her mother.

We can be friends, too, Merida thought, smiling at Orla. *Actually, we will most definitely be friends!* she decided.

As everyone rode back to DunBroch, Merida committed to starting a friendship with Orla.

Unfortunately, Orla was making it hard to get to know her.

Every question Merida asked, Orla answered in one or two words.

"Were you comfortable on your trip?" Merida asked.

"Yes," said Orla.

"Is this the farthest you've ever traveled?"

"Yes," said Orla again.

And yet, Orla chattered nonstop with Cat.

"This was your first time leaving Cardonagh, wasn't it, Orla?" asked Cat.

"Yes, it was!" Orla replied. "It was so exciting! I didn't even know a ship could be so big. Or how long two weeks could be when you're stuck on a ship. Or how hard it would be to find my sea legs."

If Merida tried to join their conversation, Orla found a way to change the subject.

"What was your favorite part of being at sea?" Merida asked.

"Oh, I don't know," Orla said, before immediately turning to Cat. "I cannot wait to take a real bath! It's been so long. How about you, Cat? How excited are you to wash your hair in clean, unsalty water? And to relax and soak in a tub for as long as you want?"

After a while, Merida gave up. She slowed Angus a bit and let Cat and Orla take the lead.

"Ach! This isn't how I planned it," Merida whispered to Angus. Angus neighed in response.

Merida rode on in silence for a few moments. But then she spied something in the distance that she had to show Cat.

She urged Angus onward and pushed between Cat's horse and Orla's. "Cat, look!" she said, pointing toward a huge apple tree. "Remember that?"

Cat's face broke into a grin. "That's the apple tree where we met!" she cried.

Angus tossed his head at the mention of the tree. He loved those apples!

"Cat told me how you met," Orla said.

"She said you're a skilled archer."

"The best archer I've ever seen!" Cat laughed.

"When did you learn to shoot?" Orla asked.

Merida remembered how Orla had been quick to exclude her from the conversation earlier. *It would only be fair if I do the same now,* she thought.

But Mum always said it was a princess's responsibility to be gracious and welcoming. So Merida replied, "I learned to shoot when I was a wee lass. My dad got me a bow for my birthday."

As they rode, Merida learned that Orla's father had died while she was still a baby. "It was just me and Mum," Orla explained, "until Mum married Braden." She stopped to smile at Cat. "That's when things got less lonely for me."

"I know what it's like to be lonely, too,"

Cat said. "That's why I'm so lucky to have met Merida." She reached for Merida's hand. "I can't wait for my new cousin and my best friend to get to know each other. I just know you'll be great friends, too!"

Orla nodded. "I agree. I've heard so much about you since the wedding, Merida. It's almost like I know you already!"

Soon, the games field came into view. Merida gazed at the banquet she'd organized and felt very proud. "Come on," she said to the other girls. She was eager to show off her hard work.

As they approached the table, Elinor hollered, "Merida, let's start the banquet!"

Fiona added, "Come along, Orla. We must take our seats."

"Coming, Mum," Orla said. She explained to

the girls, "I have to sit next to my mother. It's the proper thing to do." The way she rolled her eyes at the word "proper" made Merida think she and Orla really could get along.

"We'll see you after the meal," Merida said. Then she turned to Cat. "I saved you a chair next to me. That way, we can catch up." She just knew her friend would be happy that she'd thought of everything.

But Cat frowned. "Umm. I'm sorry, but I promised Orla that I'd sit with her. She's new here, you see, and I don't want her to be all alone."

Merida gritted her teeth but forced herself to smile. "That's fine," she answered. "I suppose I can rearrange some chairs so Orla can sit with us as well."

"Perfect!" Cat said.

But now Orla frowned. "You heard my mother. I have to sit next to her. She's very strict about things like this."

While the girls talked, everyone else went to their seats. Fiona sat in the seat that Merida had prepared for Lord Braden. Fergus and Elinor went to their chairs on one side of the table.

But there were still three empty chairs next to Fiona. *Maybe Mum won't mind if I don't sit in my regular seat,* Merida thought.

Before she could propose that they all sit together, one of Fiona's advisors sat down in one of the empty seats. Now the only spots left at the table were Merida's normal place next to Elinor and the two chairs by Fiona.

Orla quickly sat down in one of the two empty chairs near Fiona, looked at Cat, and patted the seat next to her. Cat shrugged. "Sorry, Merida," she said. "We'll talk after we eat."

"It's fine," Merida said halfheartedly. And even though she was surrounded by a table full of people, she felt very alone all of a sudden.

Chapter 3

"The banquet we are about to enjoy was planned by my daughter," Elinor announced.

Everyone clapped in approval. Merida grinned but felt her cheeks growing hot. She was both proud and embarrassed by the attention.

But when she looked toward Cat, she saw that her friend wasn't clapping. She wasn't even looking at Merida like everyone else was. Instead, she was whispering something into Orla's ear. The two of them erupted in a fit of giggles.

All through the banquet, Merida watched Cat and Orla chatting and laughing. No matter how hard she tried to catch Cat's eye, her friend was too absorbed by Orla to notice.

"You know Cat's not ignoring you, right?" Elinor whispered into Merida's ear.

"I know that," Merida grumbled.

"I think I know what you need," Elinor stated. She stood up and gestured for everyone's attention. "Excuse me," she said.

Merida didn't know what Mum was going to do. *I hope it's not a speech*, she thought.

"I have something to say to all of you," the queen began.

Merida's heart dropped. It *was* a speech.

"Occasions like this call for a speech." Elinor paused, and winked at Merida. "However, we are not just here to eat and listen to lectures. We are here to celebrate and bond with our new friends from Cardonagh!"

"Hear, hear!" King Fergus cried.

"Merida has organized many games for our enjoyment," the queen continued. "Fergus, would you go judge some of the competitions?" She leaned in to whisper to him. "Without trying to participate yourself and throwing out your back again?"

Fergus grinned sheepishly. "Yes, dear. Just judging. No competing."

"Lady Fiona," Elinor said next, "would you join me in judging the dance competition?"

"That would be lovely," Fiona said. She leaned over to her daughter. "You should stay close to me. That way I won't worry about you."

Orla blushed. Merida felt bad for her—no one liked it when parents were clingy, especially in front of other people.

"Aunt Fiona is very protective of Orla," Cat whispered. "Too protective."

Elinor must have seen Orla's embarrassment.

She said, "Maybe Orla would have more fun with Cat and Merida? Would it be all right if my daughter were to personally guarantee there is nothing to worry about?"

Orla's face lit up. Fiona frowned, but then nodded. "Of course, Queen Elinor."

Elinor smiled. "Merida, can you take the girls out to the archery challenge in the highlands?" she said, winking at her daughter.

Merida's face brightened. Mum was brilliant! Archery always made Merida happy, and Mum had just effortlessly given her time with Cat!

Elinor raised her glass and announced, "Let the celebrations begin!"

Merida all but vaulted over the table to get to Cat's side. "Are you ready?" she asked breathlessly.

"I've been practicing, so I'm sure to beat you," Cat teased.

"Wonderful!" Merida replied. "I've already prepared a bow for you." Then she paused. Orla was standing silently next to them.

"You can share my bow, Orla," she offered.

But Orla shook her head. "I think my mother expects me to stay on the games field. Besides, I'm afraid I have no talent with a bow. I'd only embarrass myself." Orla sighed. "I guess you two can go ahead."

"If you insist!" Merida said, grabbing Cat's hand to lead her back to the stables.

But Cat held back. "I really want to go with you, Merida," she said, "but we can't just leave Orla here. Can't we all do something together?"

Merida took a deep breath. Orla was guddling everything! But Cat looked so torn about what to do. Merida knew she needed to make it easier for her. "Why don't we plan on attending the archery challenge later? We could just go for a ride for now instead."

"What a wonderful idea, Merida!" Cat said.

"I love riding!" Orla exclaimed. "But my mother . . ."

"Come on, we won't ride for long," Merida said. "The quicker we leave, the quicker we'll be back." She just wanted to go. Why couldn't Orla make up her mind?

Orla looked nervous. "I guess it would be fine."

Even though there was no archery, Merida felt happier out in the open highlands of

DunBroch. "Let's ride to the Crone's Tooth," she suggested. "It's one of my favorite places."

When they reached the towering rock, Merida said, "I've climbed the Crone's Tooth and taken a drink from the Fire Falls. Legend says that only the bravest kings would do that." She winked at Cat. "The bravest princesses, too."

"Michty me!" Cat said. "Impressive!"

Merida grinned. But then she heard Orla's voice.

"Don't we have something higher to climb in Cardonagh?" she asked.

Merida blinked a few times. She was too shocked to speak. What kind of a thing to say was that?

But Cat clearly didn't think it was rude.

"I think you're right," she said. "Fionn's Column is higher."

Orla smiled. "I thought so. And I climbed that when I was a wee lass!"

Merida fought back a frown. She was about to say something, but Cat beat her to it.

"But Fionn's Column is nowhere near this sheer," Cat said. "There are lots of outcrops to use to climb there. But I hardly see any way to climb this rock!"

"You're right," Orla agreed.

"It takes skill, but I could teach you how to get to the top of the Crone's Tooth, Cat," Merida said. She turned to Orla and smirked. "You, too, Orla. Probably."

Orla scowled. She guided her horse to a different face of the Crone's Tooth.

Merida noticed Orla moving away. But she was still upset with her, so she ignored her and said, "I should have brought you here on your last trip, Cat."

Cat nodded. "It's really beautiful."

Suddenly, Orla shouted, "There's something here!"

Merida's imagination went wild as she and Cat galloped to Orla's side. She knew how to handle herself in the lands she grew up in. But she also knew there was danger here. "What is it?" she gasped.

"I don't know," Orla said, peering deeply into the woods. "Look there!" she cried.

When Merida looked, she saw a flickering blue light that she immediately recognized as a will o' the wisp.

Chapter
4

The wisps had led Merida on many adventures. But wisps also led to problems. The last thing she wanted today was to follow a twinkling blue light!

"Do you see it?" Orla asked again, inching her horse closer.

Merida and Angus moved to block her way.

"That's a will o' the wisp, and we need to stay away from them!"

"Are they dangerous?" Orla asked.

"Well, no," Merida explained, "not really. The wisps don't hurt you. They're supposed to lead you to your fate. But sometimes they lead you to places you don't want to go."

"How do you know I won't want to go where they lead?" Orla asked.

Merida's jaw clenched in frustration. Why did Orla second-guess everything? "Because I've dealt with them before," she answered, "and I know what I'm talking about."

Cat remembered the wisps from her first visit to DunBroch. She understood what Merida meant. "The last time I followed the wisps, I got more than I bargained for," she warned Orla.

"Maybe we should just stay away from them."

"Besides," Merida snapped, "don't you have to get back to your mother? Let's go."

The look on Orla's face made it clear that she'd been stung by Merida's words. "I didn't mean to—" Merida started.

But then a wisp popped up in front of Orla's face, and she was off. "I have to see where they come from!" she shouted.

"We have to go after her!" Cat cried. She began to chase Orla.

"Oh, Angus," Merida complained. "I hope this doesn't turn into a catastrophe!"

Merida and Angus were used to racing through the highlands. Most of the time, they could outrun any horse and rider. But today, in pursuit of the wisps, Orla spurred her mount to a pace that Merida and Angus couldn't match.

So far, Merida had been able to keep Orla within sight. But the wisps were heading deep into the woods. She didn't want to lose Orla among the trees. "Come on, Cat!" she shouted.

They rode down the path behind Orla. Somehow, though, the trees seemed to melt away. The girls found themselves on the edge of a clearing. Orla had dismounted from her horse and approached a cottage.

"Ach!" Merida muttered under her breath. "Not this again."

Merida knew this house—it belonged to the googly old Witch. Things never turned out as planned when the Witch was involved. Wisps plus Witch would most certainly equal disaster!

"What a lovely cottage," Orla said.

Merida quickly stepped between Orla and the house. She put her hands up and said, "We should go. We don't want to be accused of trespassing, and it looks like the place is abandoned anyway."

Orla scowled and brushed past her. "Why do we have to be worried about trespassing if it's abandoned?"

"That's a good point," Cat said. "Exploring

might be fun. And Orla's mother is so strict, she almost never gets a chance to explore."

Cat pointed at a sign near the cottage door. "It says THE CRAFTY CARVER. And there's something else." She leaned in close and read, "'Most Favored Woodcarver of Princess Merida.'"

"So you've known whose cottage this is the whole time?" Orla asked.

Merida gulped. "Please, trust me," she said. "You don't want to go in there."

Orla's eyes narrowed as she reached for the door. "It's hard to trust someone who doesn't tell us the whole story."

Merida clenched her fists, then followed the other girls into the cottage. After all, she couldn't let them face the Witch alone. "Maybe she won't be home," she muttered.

Inside, Cat and Orla examined the Witch's carvings, which were still very bear-related. Merida looked for any sign of the old woman or her talking crow. It seemed like her wish might have come true—the house looked empty.

"These are adorable!" Cat squealed, holding up some wooden bear puppets. "Should we buy a few for the triplets?"

"Yes!" Orla cried.

"Well, the wood-carver isn't here," Merida said, "so we can't." She tried to usher the girls out of the cottage. "Let's get back to the horses."

As she spoke, an old woman walked into the room. "Hello, hello!" she said. "You holler if you see anything you like. Everything is half off."

"Who are you?" Cat asked.

"She's the wood-carver," Merida replied.

"Let's buy those puppets and go—"

But the woman interrupted. "Actually, I'm a Witch."

Merida's jaw dropped open. She couldn't believe it! "You're not a Witch," she sputtered. "You're a *wood-carver*! Like you *always* tell me!"

"Witch!" the woman shouted.

"Wood-carver!" Merida answered.

"Merida!" Orla cried. "If she says she's a Witch, she's a Witch!"

The Witch crossed her arms and nodded. "Now, what can I do for you wee lasses?"

"What kinds of spells do you have?" Orla asked gleefully.

"No no no!" Merida hollered. "We don't want any spells. Really." She snatched up a carved bear figurine. "I'll buy this. Actually, I'll buy three of them! And I'll pay full price!"

But the Witch wasn't listening. She was rummaging through a shelf under the counter. "Where is it?" she mumbled. "Here!" She grinned and got up, holding a box. "Come take a closer look," she said, and threw open the lid.

Merida didn't expect the box to be filled with about a dozen . . . red and blue berries?

Even Orla looked confused. "Those aren't spells," she said. "Are they?"

"It looks like your breakfast to me," Cat added. "Can I have a strawberry?"

The Witch looked outraged. She pulled the box back and snapped, "No! And don't judge a thing by what it looks like."

"You're right," Orla soothed. "We were being silly. What kind of spells are these?" She smiled sweetly, and the Witch's frown changed into a small smile. She even pushed the box closer to the girls so they could see.

"I think we should go," Merida said, looking directly at Cat. "You know what magic can do if you're not careful."

Cat shrugged. "It can't hurt to *look*," she said. "We're not going to buy any."

Merida's heart sank as Cat and Orla crowded around the box.

"Well, this one," the Witch said, pointing at the first berry, a black currant, "is a strength spell. This spell gives you speed. And this one is a beauty spell." She went through each of the berries in order. "This is a spell for good luck, this one here is a binding spell, this one is a spell to make you taller, and this takes away bad breath."

When she was done, Orla asked, "Are the spells for sale?"

Merida couldn't stay silent any longer. "We're not buying any spells!" she cried. "It's time for us to go home to DunBroch." She pointed toward the door, hoping the girls would exit.

But instead, Orla scowled. "You can't order me around," she said.

"Ach! I'm not ordering you around!" Merida said. Why was everything so hard with Orla? "Magic and spells aren't for fun. There can be serious consequences!"

This time, Cat was on Merida's side. "I thought we were just going to look, Orla," she said. "Merida is right about the dangers of magic—especially magic we don't understand. We should leave the spells alone."

Orla's scowl transformed into more of a pout. Merida could tell she really wanted a spell from the Witch. But eventually, she stammered, "I—I suppose you're right." She walked away to look at some of the carvings near the door. Cat followed her.

Merida breathed a sigh of relief.

Until the Witch started yelling.

"Don't get in the way of my sales, lassie!" she yelped, shaking her finger at Merida. "Let her buy a spell. I remember *you* once did the same."

"Yes," Merida replied, "and I remember how much trouble that decision caused!"

The Witch glared at her. "Now, which spell would you like?" she said, turning to Orla. But Orla was gone! "Where did she go?"

"She's outside. She said we convinced her to

leave the spells alone," Cat said. "See, Merida? It all worked out."

Merida rolled her eyes. "I think we've talked enough about spells." She walked over to the spell box to close it. But then she noticed something strange. Cat had mentioned a strawberry in the box, but Merida couldn't see one.

She must have been wrong, Merida thought, shaking her head and slamming the lid shut.

When Cat and Merida said good-bye, the Witch called after them. "Just a moment, dearies."

Merida looked over her shoulder. What did she want now?

The Witch held up the bear figurines from earlier. "You still owe me for three of these, Princess. You did say full price, right?"

Orla sulked the entire ride back to DunBroch.

Which meant Cat spent the entire ride trying to cheer her up.

Which meant Merida was left out *again*.

Nothing changed when they got home, either. "How about we all go inside for something to eat," Merida suggested.

Orla answered, "I'd prefer to be outside."

Merida took a deep breath. "Fine. There are still competitions at the games field," she said. "We could watch the strength contests. Really, anything except dancing. Watching other people dance is boring, and I can't dance at all."

"Dancing!" Orla cried. "My mother is judging the dancing!" She bit her lip. "I should get over there."

Merida's teeth clenched. Didn't Orla just hear her say she hated dancing?

Cat looked from Merida to Orla. "There's nothing else you want to do?" she asked.

Orla sighed. "You know that's where my mother expects me to be."

"You're right," Cat agreed. "We can teach

you how to dance, Merida."

"No, you two go ahead. I'll just watch," Merida said flatly.

Cat and Orla joined the dancers. Merida trailed behind, still upset that every time she tried to do something with Cat, Orla managed to ruin it.

Elinor and Fiona were seated on a dais nearby, judging the dancers. When Mum spotted Merida, she motioned for her to join them.

"Is my daughter still with you?" Lady Fiona asked. She sounded so stern that Merida began to understand why Orla was nervous while they were riding. "She's just dancing over there," Merida answered, pointing.

"Don't you want to dance, too, Merida?" Elinor asked.

"You know I don't like dancing," Merida mumbled.

"I've taught Orla to love dancing," Fiona said. "All ladies should know how to dance."

"Merida, maybe you should try something new," Mum suggested. "Cat and Orla look like they're having fun."

That was the last thing Merida wanted to hear. "I just want to sit," she said. She wandered over to an empty bench. *Nothing is working out the way I planned,* she thought. *I wanted to have time with my friend. Instead, I'm all alone.*

"Hear, hear!" Elinor announced. "Lady Fiona has agreed to teach everyone the traditional Cardonagh jig. Let's have a group dancing lesson!" Fiona rose and the crowd assembled.

Merida spotted three familiar flashes of red

on the far edge of the crowd. Even the triplets had come to dance. The boys found the one muddy patch to dance on instead of dry soil. They were doing their best to hop and toe-tap in time. But all they really managed to do was cover themselves with mud.

That gave Merida an idea.

She quietly positioned herself behind a tree near the triplets. "Boys!" she hissed. "Come over here, please!"

Harris, Hubert, and Hamish scurried over at the sound of their sister's voice. The triplets could certainly be a handful, and they caused Merida a lot of trouble. But no one could deny how much they loved their big sister. They were always ready to help her if asked—especially if a bribe was involved.

"I need a favor," Merida whispered. Her face broke into a slow smile. "I have a present for each of you if you can help me get some time with Cat by myself, without Orla."

The triplets furrowed their brows. They didn't know what Merida meant, but they were curious.

"You three are covered in mud," Merida continued. "What if you *accidentally* ran into Orla?"

Harris raised his eyebrows. Hubert and Hamish tilted their heads.

"After all," Merida explained, "Orla loves baths! Earlier, she couldn't stop talking about how much she loves to soak in a tub." That much, at least, was true.

The triplets looked at one another for a moment. Finally, Harris nodded for all three of them.

"Wonderful!" Merida cried. "Go on, then." She pointed to Orla, who was still dancing a jig.

But the boys didn't move.

Merida scratched her head. "What's wrong?" she asked.

On cue, her brothers each held out a hand. Immediately, Merida understood.

"You rascals," she said. "Can't you just do this

for your big sister?"

All three shook their heads.

Merida sighed. "I did promise you a present."
She reached into her pocket and took out the
figurines from the Witch's cottage. "Will these
do?"

The boys' eyes lit up. They snatched the toys
and ran off to find Orla.

The boys were absolutely disgusting. They
smelled worse than piglets or five-day-old
haggis. Even Merida, who didn't mind getting
dirty from time to time, didn't want to touch
them.

That's when she realized how horrible her
plan was. *How could I have sent them to smear that
mess all over Orla? It's just not right!*

She started running. "Hamish!" she shouted.

"Harris! Hubert!"

But her voice was drowned out by the music being played for the dancers.

She snaked her way through the crowd, trying to get to Orla first. But the swarm of dancers blocked her path.

She caught a glimpse of mud and red curls. The boys were about to charge into Orla. Merida had to warn her! "Orla!" she yelled. "Watch out!"

"What?" Orla said, taking a step toward Merida. "Watch out for what?"

Merida finally reached her and positioned herself to block her brothers from getting to Orla. "Watch out for the triplets!" she yelped.

Orla had stepped out of the way, but Cat was still in the boys' path. They ran by like a tornado of mud, smearing grime all over her. Then, unaware they'd mucked the wrong girl, the triplets continued on their way to the castle.

The commotion didn't escape Elinor's attention. "Boys!" she yelled from the dais. "When I catch the three of you, I'm going to boil your heads!"

"Crivens!" Cat shouted. "What just happened?" She looked down at her dress and her braids. There was mud everywhere.

Merida lowered her eyes. "I'm sorry, Cat. I didn't mean—"

But Orla interrupted her. "Were you trying to warn *me* about your brothers?" Her eyes narrowed. "How did you know they were going to get me dirty?"

Now Merida looked down at the ground. "It—it was stupid," she stammered. "I just thought maybe . . . if the boys . . . all I wanted . . ."

"*You* sent them to do this?" Cat shrieked. "On purpose?"

"I'm really sorry!" Merida cried. "It's just that I've missed you so much and I've barely been able to speak to you since you've been here!"

"I cannot believe you would do something so mean and selfish!" Orla snapped. "Come on, Cat. I'll help you get cleaned up." She reached for Cat's hand.

But Cat yanked it away. "You know what? Merida's not the only one who's been unfriendly today. It's clear to me you haven't wanted to get to know her at all."

Orla's mouth hung open. "I—I—" she

stuttered, not knowing what to say.

But Cat held up a muddy hand. "Just stop. You both are pretending to be kind right now. But really, you're bickering and pulling me in two different directions."

Merida glanced at Orla. Then she lowered her eyes again, feeling ashamed.

"Are you girls all right?" Elinor shouted from the dais.

"We're fine!" Cat answered. "I just need to go wash up." She looked at Merida and Orla. "Alone."

Cat took a few steps away. Then she looked back and said, "I really thought the two of you would be friends. Or at least that you'd give each other a chance. I'm sorry I was wrong."

Chapter 6

As soon as Cat was out of sight, Merida glared at Orla. "Now she's mad at both of us," she hissed. "This is all *your* fault!"

"*My* fault?" Orla shouted. "You're the one who created this mess! Literally!"

"Yes, but you've spent the day picking fights with me!" Merida answered.

"I have not! You've been trying to order me around all day. All I've done is stand up for myself," Orla said. "You don't even care what I want to do or how much trouble I could get in just because I've gone along with your ideas!" She spun on her heel to follow Cat. But as she did so, a red item fell out of her pocket.

"What is that?" Merida asked. Something about it was very familiar.

Orla tried to shove the item back into her pocket. But Merida grabbed her hand—and she saw exactly what it was.

"Is this a spell? From the Witch?" Merida asked.

Orla pulled her hand away. "So what if it is?" she snapped.

"Did you steal it?" Merida demanded.

"I don't want to talk about it!" Orla yelled.

She tried to go, but Merida grasped her sleeve and pulled her behind a haystack. She didn't want Mum or anyone else to see Orla's stolen spell. "You can't just steal a spell from a Witch!" Merida shrieked. "Give it to me *now*!"

Orla glared at Merida with a look of pure anger. And then, before Merida could stop her, she plopped the strawberry into her mouth and swallowed it in one gulp.

"What did you do?" Merida gasped.

Orla didn't answer. Instead, she fell to her knees coughing.

Merida remembered giving Elinor one of the Witch's spells. Mum had reacted in this same way. Suddenly, her heart was pounding. What if Orla had stolen the same spell?

Merida crouched down by Orla and asked, "What spell did you take?" She silently wished that it wasn't a spell to change her fate.

Between coughs, Orla gasped, "It was just a beauty spell."

I hope that googly old crone doesn't think bears are beautiful, Merida thought. She held out her hand. "Come on," she said, "let me help you up."

Orla took Merida's hand. "Thank you," she said as she got back on her feet.

"You're welcome," Merida said. "Do you need any other help?"

"No."

"Then why are you still holding my hand?"

"What?" Orla looked confused. She jerked her hand away to free herself from Merida's grip—but all she managed to do was to pull Merida off balance. Both girls landed in a tangled heap on the ground. But their hands remained attached. All five of Merida's fingers and her entire palm seemed to be glued to Orla's hand.

"Let go, Orla!" Merida shouted.

"You let go!" Orla shouted back.

Merida's eyes widened. "The spell!" she cried. "It wasn't the beauty spell! It was the *binding* spell!"

Merida knew they were in trouble. Magic

had a way of complicating everything. "We have to break this spell," she gasped. But first, they needed to get away from the games field. If anyone found out about this, she'd never be allowed out of DunBroch again!

But the only way out was to pass the dais . . . where Elinor was.

"Listen," Merida hissed, "my parents can't find out about this spell. Especially Mum. She would *not* be happy."

"Fine by me," Orla replied, "as long as my mother doesn't find out, either. I'd be in so much trouble." Her voice dropped to a mumble. "I'm probably already in trouble for something."

Merida glanced at Orla out of the corner of her eye. Maybe Orla understood what it was like to love your mother even though she drove you crazy from time to time.

But there was no time to think about that, not until they broke this stupid spell. "Let's go back to the castle," Merida suggested. "Then we can figure out what to do."

Because of the way their hands were bound, they had two choices—Merida could put her arm behind Orla and around her waist, or Merida's arm could go in front, making it look as if the girls were holding hands. "Hand-holding is less unbelievable than hugging," Orla said.

Merida nodded. "Just try not to attract any attention," she snapped.

The girls forced themselves to walk as normally as possible. As they neared the dais, Merida pretended that she was giving Orla a tour of DunBroch. "That's a birch tree," she said, pointing with her free hand. "And over there, we have a fine highland sheep."

Elinor and Fiona looked over their shoulders as the girls passed. "What are you two doing?" Elinor asked, arching an eyebrow.

"Merida is giving me a tour of DunBroch," Orla answered. "There are so many things I've never seen before!"

Now Fiona looked skeptical. "We have sheep at Cardonagh, Orla," she said.

Orla shrugged.

"Are you two holding hands?" Elinor asked.

Merida should have known Mum would notice. She bit her lip, not knowing what to say.

But Orla had an idea. "We've become dear, dear friends," she said, smiling.

"I suppose that's good news," Mum said. But

her eyes narrowed with suspicion.

It was time to get out of there. Merida waved good-bye with her free hand. "We have to be off. We're meeting Cat at the castle. See you later!"

When they reached Merida's bedroom, she slammed the door shut and then turned on Orla. "How could you be so reckless?" she asked through gritted teeth.

"Me?" Orla yelled. "Are you blaming *me* for this?"

"Who else? *You* stole the spell. *You* ate the spell. *You* got us stuck together!"

Orla tried throwing her hands in the air—but only managed to get one up. Merida stubbornly held her right hand down so that Orla's left hand wouldn't move. Orla glared and said, "I never would have eaten that stupid berry if *you* hadn't been so insufferable!"

"What did *I* do?" Merida demanded.

Orla laughed, but it wasn't a happy laugh. "It's so obvious you don't want me here. You had a seat saved for Cat at the banquet. You had a bow ready for her. You set up an archery challenge for her." She looked away. "You didn't want to include me in any of that."

Merida's eyes grew wide. "But I didn't even know you were coming!" she explained. But then it hit her—everything Orla was saying was true. She thought she'd hidden her feelings, but she really *didn't* want Orla here.

Merida didn't have any time to explain, though. Someone was knocking loudly on her bedroom door.

"We're going to get caught!" Orla whispered, looking panicked.

Merida could hardly breathe. There was another knock. Then someone said, "Are you in there, Merida?"

Merida sighed with relief. "It's only Cat." She opened the door and pulled Cat inside.

"What are you doing?" Cat asked. "Why are you two *holding hands*?" Her face lit up with a smile. "Did you figure out how to be friends?"

"It's a long story," Orla started.

"Orla stole a spell from the Witch and it was a binding spell and now we're magically bound together and we don't know what to do!" Merida explained.

Cat's mouth dropped open. "Orla! We agreed we wouldn't touch the spells!"

Orla hung her head. "I know. It was childish. I was just so annoyed when everyone was telling me what to do. I just wanted to do the opposite."

"How did you get from stealing the spell to using the spell?" Cat asked.

Merida looked away. "That's partly my fault. After you left, we argued. We both lost our temper, and it just happened."

Cat sighed. "What do we do now?"

"We have to break the spell," Orla said.

"But how?" Cat asked.

"We go back to the Witch," Merida said. Her mouth was set in a grim line. "And we hope she can make this right."

Chapter 7

"We have to get out of here without anyone seeing us," Merida declared. She opened the bedroom door slowly, making sure the hallway was empty.

The girls tiptoed through the castle. To keep their sticky situation a secret, they needed to get to the stables as quickly as possible. The shortest way was through the dining hall.

"Are you sure we won't get caught?" Cat asked.

Merida shook her head. "The evening banquet will be held outside on the games field again. The dining hall should be empty."

As Merida predicted, except for some plates of leftover food, the room was deserted. The girls hurried through. But when Orla suddenly froze, Merida jerked to a stop.

"What are you doing?" Merida asked.

"I just want a treat," Orla said, grabbing a drumstick from a platter and taking a bite. Then she giggled. "Hey, Cat," she said while chewing. "I wonder what my mother would say right now?"

Cat smiled. In her best formal Fiona voice, she said, "A lady shouldn't—"

But Merida finished her sentence. "—stuff her gob!"

"How did you know that?" Orla asked.

Now it was Merida's turn to giggle. "Because *my* mother says that to me *all the time*!"

Orla passed drumsticks to Merida and Cat. "Go ahead and stuff your gobs, too!"

They gathered around the table, eating quickly and not expecting to be interrupted.

"Merida!" Fergus whined. "I stole those drumsticks for myself!" The king chuckled. "I should have known not to leave them unattended."

Dad's eyes moved from Merida's face to her hand clasping Orla's. Merida had to do something to keep him from getting suspicious. She just didn't know what.

Suddenly, Orla yanked Merida's arm down to the tabletop and said, "I'm going to show you which one of us is the arm wrestling champion!"

Merida was caught off guard. How did Orla think of a believable cover story so quickly? She propped up on her elbow and said, "I'm ready when you are!"

"But your hands are all wrong," Fergus said, scratching his head.

He was right. Because the girls couldn't change how their hands were stuck together, their wrists were bent awkwardly.

"This is how we arm wrestle in Cardonagh," Cat explained. "It's more challenging this way." She grinned at Fergus.

Dad shrugged. "I suppose that makes sense," he said. "Have fun, girls. I'm going to take the rest of my snack with me back to the games field. That way no one else will steal it!"

When Fergus was gone, Merida let out a sigh of relief. Then she said, "Good thinking, Orla. You, too, Cat. I thought our secret was out for sure!"

"Well, let's find the Witch and get rid of the secret for good," Orla said.

That was the best idea Merida had heard so far!

Merida thought she knew the way through the highlands to the Witch's cottage. But no matter where she looked, the cottage was nowhere to be found.

Merida brought Angus to a halt. "It was here earlier!" she said, jumping off Angus's back to better explore the wooded forest—and bringing Orla crashing down with her.

"Oof!" Orla grunted.

"I'm so sorry!" Merida cried. "I forgot!" She helped Orla to stand and brush the leaves off her dress.

Cat dismounted her horse as well. But instead of checking to see if Orla was all right, she headed for the woods. Then she shouted, "Look!" as she pointed into the trees. "Is that a wisp?"

There was a flash of twinkling blue light deep in the woods. "The wisps led me to the Witch's cottage before," Orla said. "Maybe we should follow them again."

The trees and bushes here were too thick for horses. They'd have to continue on foot.

"I don't see any other way," Cat said.

"I hope this works," Merida groaned.

Normally, Merida could scurry through the forests of DunBroch as easily as she walked the halls of the castle. But trying to climb over rocks and push between tree trunks was a lot harder with another person attached to your hand.

"How far into the woods are the wisps going to take us?" she muttered.

"I'd be happy if there were fewer thorns along the way," Orla replied.

"You two are so slow," Cat teased. "Try to keep up!"

Merida and Orla both scowled. "I can't wait until we break this spell," Orla said, "so I can race

Cat for real."

"Absolutely!" Merida agreed.

The wisps soon snaked through an open field. That made it easier to travel—and to talk.

"How did you meet the Witch in the first place?" Orla asked.

Merida took a deep breath. "Ach!" she said. "It was when I wanted something to change my mother. The Witch gave me a spell, but it didn't work out at all like I wanted."

"What happened?" Cat asked.

"Let's just say Mum can be a real bear when we're fighting!" Merida giggled.

Orla laughed. "It's good to know that there are other girls who don't always get along with their mothers."

"That's putting it mildly," Merida drawled.

"Do you know why I'm not good with a bow and arrow?" Orla asked.

Merida shook her head.

"Because Aunt Fiona won't let her practice archery until her sewing is perfect." Cat snickered.

"And my sewing is never perfect," Orla lamented.

"It sounds like our mothers could be twins," Merida said, arching an eyebrow.

"Oh, I hope not!" Orla cried. "One of her is more than enough!"

Merida laughed. Orla had just described how Merida felt about her mum. There was no one she loved more than her mother—but there was only so much Mum she could handle!

"You know," Cat said, "one of the things that

drew me to Orla when we first met was how much she reminded me of you, Merida."

Merida hadn't thought about that. She lowered her eyes to the ground. She'd been so busy being jealous of Orla that she hadn't tried to get to know her. She took a deep breath and announced, "I need to say something to you both."

When no one answered, Merida raised her eyes. "Did you hear me?" she asked.

But then she realized why both Orla and Cat were silent. They were transfixed by the sudden appearance of a swarm of flickering blue lights.

"Wisps!" Merida gasped. "So many of them!" Her heart started to pound. "They must be trying to show us something."

Usually, the wisps formed a trail that would

lead to treasure . . . or doom. But instead of leading somewhere, the cloud of wisps drifted closer—but only to Merida and Orla. Soon the dancing blue lights encircled them.

"What does it mean?" Orla asked.

Merida was so frustrated that her free hand curled into a fist. "It means that your fate"—she took a ragged breath—"your fate is with me. And my fate is with you." She slowly exhaled. "You and I are fated to be together—forever."

Chapter
8

"You don't know that, Merida," Cat said. "The wisps are mysterious."

"It's the only thing that makes sense." Merida sighed. "We might as well give up."

"Give up?" Orla asked, shaking her head. "That's not the Merida I've heard about."

"And it's not the Merida I know," Cat added.

"We don't even know where we are!" Merida shouted. "What can we do?"

Orla lifted her bound hand up over her head, forcing Merida to do the same. That allowed her to look Merida in the eye under the arc of their arms. "You are Princess Merida of DunBroch," she said. "These are your lands. You know where everything is. I know you can find the Witch's cottage. I believe in you."

"I believe in you, too," Cat said. "Don't give up!"

Merida's eyes clouded with tears. "Thank you for saying that." She twisted around so she was hugging Orla from behind, then gestured for Cat to come closer. The three girls hugged for a moment.

When they stepped away, Merida's jaw

dropped. The wisps that had just been circling around them had separated. Once again, the lights formed a snaking path through the woods.

Merida beamed. "Come on!" she shouted.

The girls ran to follow the wisps. But this time, it was easier for Merida and Orla. Each paid more attention to the other, and there was less staggering and stumbling, even through the heavy woods.

Just as before, the trees suddenly seemed to melt away. The girls were left standing in a clearing, lit by a single blue wisp.

"Look!" Merida cried. "The Witch's cottage!"

The three girls grinned and hurried to the door, but it opened before they could knock.

"Back so soon, lassies?" the Witch asked from the doorway. "If you need more carvings,

I have plenty!" She gestured around her workshop.

"We don't want to buy carvings," Merida said. "We need to buy . . . a spell. Or at least, the cure to a spell." She pointed down at her hand. "We need to break a binding spell."

"Where did you find a binding spell?" the Witch asked. "Those are rare." She began to rummage under the counter again. "In fact, I only have one."

Merida shut her eyes. She knew what was coming.

The Witch opened her spell box. "My binding spell!" she shouted. "It's missing!"

Now Orla gulped. "I—I stole it," she admitted.

"You did *what?*" The Witch's face

transformed from kindly to chilling. Merida instinctively took a step backward, dragging Orla with her.

"I'm s-sorry," Orla sputtered. "I know it was wrong. I don't even know why I did it!"

"Now we need your help," Cat said. "Merida and Orla are stuck together because of the binding spell. Can you tell us how to break it?"

"Please?" Merida begged.

The Witch's eyes narrowed. "You *stole* a spell from me, right under my nose," she thundered, "and now you've come for my *help*? What kind of tumshies are you?" She pointed her wand at the girls. A bright yellow ball of light formed at the tip. All three girls raised their arms to shield themselves from the blinding light. "I'm going to turn your wool into feathers!" the Witch spat.

The girls dropped their arms. "What?" Merida said.

"They're not sheep," cawed the Witch's crow.

The Witch scratched her head. "Wrong spell," she muttered, flicking her wand. Now the ball of light was pink. "From this day forth, your skin will be free of warts!"

"They're not toads," the crow squawked,

flying over to the Witch and grabbing her wand with his claws. "Give me that!" he said.

"But we don't tolerate thieves at the Crafty Carver!" She wrestled with her crow over the wand. "I should turn them all into field mice! Or worms!"

"Please!" Merida cried again. "Orla was wrong to steal the spell."

Orla nodded vigorously in agreement.

"She made a mistake," Merida continued. "But everyone makes mistakes. I know I have."

"Me too," Cat said.

"Haven't you ever made a mistake?" Merida asked.

The Witch lowered her wand and crossed her arms. "A bona fide witch never makes a mistake."

"Not true! Not true!" squawked the crow.

"What are you talking about?" the Witch muttered.

"Ian! Prince Ian!" the crow said.

"What happened to Prince Ian?" Cat asked.

The Witch blushed. "Little Prince Ian asked to be as big as his brother. He just wasn't planning to be turned into a hog."

The Crow shook his head in disbelief.

"Fine," the Witch said, sighing. "I suppose I've made a mistake or two."

Merida exhaled deeply. "Then you understand," she said, taking the Witch's hand. "One mistake shouldn't lead to a lifetime of punishment. But if Orla and I can't break this spell . . . well, neither of us will ever get to make a choice of our own again. We'll have to do everything together, go everywhere together. I'll never shoot a bow again."

"And I'll never play the harp again," Orla said. "Or race on horseback."

"Or climb the Crone's Tooth," Merida added. Then a slow realization hit her. There was a consequence to the spell that was worse than all the others put together. "If we can't break the spell, then either we both stay in DunBroch or we both return to Cardonagh." She gulped. "Which means one of us will lose our family."

When Merida finished speaking, tears glistened in the Witch's eyes. Even her crow seemed to be a little sniffly. "Oh, lassies," she said, first patting Merida's cheek and then Orla's. "You're right. One mistake shouldn't cause a lifetime of sorrow."

"Then you'll help them?" Cat asked, grinning.

Merida grinned as well—but then she saw the Witch's face. Something was wrong.

"I want to help," the Witch began, "I truly do. But . . . you see . . . the thing is . . ."

"Just tell us," Orla said. Her jaw was clenched. She could tell something was wrong, too.

The Witch sighed. "Binding spells are . . . permanent."

"What?" Merida cried.

The Witch nodded. "They're permanent. Unbreakable. Perpetual. Unending."

Orla gasped. "What have we done?"

Chapter 9

The three girls left the Crafty Carver's cottage as if they were in a trance, even though there was no new magic involved. Every once in a while, one of them would whisper, "I can't believe this."

None of the girls noticed the bear cub sleeping against a tree. Not until Cat was about to walk right into him.

"Crivens!" Cat cried.

Merida clapped her free hand over Cat's mouth. "Shhh!" she hissed. "We don't want to wake him!"

"What do we do now?" Orla whispered.

"Look there," Merida answered, pointing to a rocky ridge. "I recognize that path—it's a shortcut to DunBroch. Let's back away as quietly as we can and get to the ridge."

Cat and Orla both gave curt nods and began to tiptoe backward. But before they got very far, something came crashing through the woods. It was the mother bear, racing toward her cub.

"She caught our scent," Merida gasped.

"What do we do now?" Orla's eyes were

wide with terror.

"We run!" Merida replied.

The mother bear spied the human intruders. She stood over her sleepy cub, rose on her hind legs, and roared. She was so loud that the leaves on the trees shook.

The three girls raced to the ridge as fast as possible, though Merida and Orla had to side-shuffle in some places instead of running. But

they were careful to talk to each other to make sure they were going the same way.

Cat reached the path before Merida and Orla. "Keep running!" Merida yelled. She wanted Cat to get to safety as quickly as possible. Cat raced ahead and was soon out of sight.

The girls kept moving until they couldn't hear the mother bear's roars anymore. When they finally stopped, Merida was out of breath. "I think we're safe," she panted.

"I don't see or hear her," Orla agreed. "How about you, Cat? Do you see anything?"

But Cat was nowhere to be found.

"Maybe she ran farther than us," Merida said, looking around for some sign of Cat. Then she heard something. It sounded like someone was calling for help.

"Did you hear that?" Orla asked.

Merida nodded. "It's Cat!" she shouted.

The girls followed the cries. As they got closer, they easily recognized Cat's voice. They reached the crest of the ridge, which was crowned by a great gnarled oak.

"Help!" Cat yelled. "I'm down here! I stumbled while I was running away!"

Merida looked over the edge of the ridge. Then she gasped. Cat was dangling from a thick, knotted root of an oak tree. She tried finding a foothold on the cliff face, but the wall crumbled whenever she touched it.

"Hold on, Cat!" Merida shouted. Turning to Orla, she said, "We have to reach her!"

"But how?" Orla cried.

Merida bit her lip. Then she gestured for

Orla to sit down on the ridge. "If you lie on your back, I'll lie on my belly," Merida explained. "Then I'll reach down for her."

But no matter what, Merida's arms couldn't stretch enough to reach Cat. "She's too far down," Merida cried. "I can't lean any farther without losing my balance."

"I can't hold on much longer!" Cat shrieked.

"We need to get closer to her," Orla said.

"I think I have a plan," Merida replied, pointing to the oak tree. "One of us can hold on to a low branch while the other is being lowered down to get to Cat."

Orla thought for a moment. Then she nodded.

"You grab a branch," Merida said. "I'll hang over the edge to get to Cat." She winked.

"Don't let go of me, all right?"

Orla snorted. "As if I could!"

The girls got into position. Orla stretched as far over the edge as she could while still holding securely to the tree. Then Merida dangled from Orla's hand and reached down.

It was a long drop from the edge of the ridge. For the first time, Merida was happy to be permanently attached to Orla—she didn't want to worry about Orla losing her grip!

"Take my hand, Cat!" Merida shouted, straining to get closer.

Cat took a deep breath, then swung an arm toward Merida.

"I got you!" Merida cried.

Orla tugged, Merida pulled, and Cat pushed off the rocks as best she could. Together, the

three girls fought their way back onto solid ground. They moved away from the edge and collapsed onto the path. They huffed and puffed, too exhausted to speak.

That was when Merida noticed something. "Look!" she shouted. "Our thumbs! They're free!" Merida wiggled her thumb to punctuate her words.

At first, Orla's face lit up. But almost immediately, she frowned. "I don't think our thumbs were ever stuck," she said.

"No, you're wrong," Merida answered. "This is a sign that the binding spell can be broken." She looked from Orla to Cat. "It has to be," she said.

Cat shook her head. "I think Orla is right. I don't remember your thumbs being bonded."

Merida scratched her head with her free

hand. *Had* her thumb ever been stuck to Orla's hand? Or had it always been free and she was grasping at straws? She just didn't know. "Maybe you're right," she admitted miserably. She glanced down at the ground so the others wouldn't see how close she was to crying.

After a few moments, Cat took her friends' hands. "Come on, you two," she said. "Let's go back to DunBroch. Maybe someone there will know what to do."

Merida and Orla looked at each other, and Merida could tell Orla was as skeptical as she was. The Witch had already told them the binding spell was permanent. There was no one at DunBroch who would be able to do anything about that. But she forced herself to smile. Cat was trying to give them hope, and Merida appreciated her friend's effort. She nodded at Orla and gestured that they should go.

By the time they rode through the gates of Castle DunBroch, Merida had made a decision. She couldn't figure out how to break the binding spell, but she knew exactly how to take responsibility for this mess.

She just had to make her parents understand. And maybe break their hearts.

Chapter
10

Everyone at DunBroch was gathered in the Great Hall of the castle. Elinor and Fiona sat side by side on the dais. Fergus mingled with the guests, laughing and drinking.

"Are you ready?" Merida asked Orla. Orla nodded.

Cat stepped next to Merida, took her free

hand, and squeezed. "Let's go," she said.

"Cat, you're not responsible for any of this," Orla said.

"You don't need to get scolded, too," Merida added.

Cat smiled. "You two are my best friends. Do you really think I'm going to let you face this without me?" She shook her head. "We're in this together."

Merida was glad for Cat's hand to hold— and for Orla's. They walked toward the dais.

Fiona spotted the girls first. "Orla, I've been looking for you!" she cried, stretching a hand toward her daughter. "Where have you been?"

One look at her daughter's face and Elinor knew there was a problem. She rose from her seat and asked, "What's wrong?"

Merida took a deep breath. Then she said in a trembling voice, "Something happened."

Fiona sprang to her feet. She put a hand on Orla's shoulder. "Let's give Elinor and Merida some privacy. I want to talk to you alone, too." She tried to lead Orla away, but her daughter wouldn't budge.

Fiona arched an eyebrow. "I know you two have become friends," she said, "but enough hand-holding!"

"That's what we're trying to tell you!" Orla cried. "We can't stop holding hands!"

"We're bound together forever," Merida added.

"What?" Fiona asked.

Elinor looked at the girls' bound hands. She put a hand on Merida's shoulder and looked her daughter in the eye. "Tell me everything," she said. "Now."

The whole story came spilling out of Merida. The wisps. The Witch's cottage. The spell. The argument. How the three of them had tried— and failed—to break the spell. "But the Witch said binding spells are permanent," Merida moaned. "There's nothing we can do. We're stuck with each other for life."

Elinor and Fiona looked at each other. Their jaws dropped. There was a moment of silence.

And then the yelling began.

"How could you do something so foolish?" Fiona demanded.

"How many times do you have to toy with magic before you learn not to?" Elinor asked.

Elinor grabbed Merida's free hand while Fiona grabbed Orla's. The two ladies pulled as hard as they could. But Merida's hand remained firmly stuck to Orla's.

The ruckus got Fergus's attention. "What is all this commotion?" he bellowed, stepping onto the dais. The triplets also quietly came closer, eager to hear what was going on.

By now, everyone was watching the antics on the dais.

"Our daughter," Elinor answered, "got herself into another mess!"

"No, she didn't!" Orla shouted. "Don't be angry at Merida. This was all my fault. I stole from the Witch. I used a spell I didn't understand."

"Actually," Cat said, "Merida tried to warn us. We didn't listen."

Elinor looked stunned. She wasn't expecting such a fierce defense!

Merida wasn't, either. She gulped. Only true friends would stand up for her like this.

Then Fiona roared, "I cannot believe you could be this irresponsible, Orla! This is why I don't like you to go off on your own. I have to watch over you every moment!"

Orla hung her head while her mother yelled. She didn't say a word to defend herself.

So it was up to Merida.

"Lady Fiona," Merida said, "this wasn't all Orla's fault, either. In fact, I'm more responsible than she is. I didn't really make her feel welcome. She didn't know why the Witch's spells could be dangerous, and I didn't explain. I just ordered her around and expected her to do as I said. Even when I saw I'd hurt her feelings, I didn't change." She took a deep breath. "If I had just been honest with her, we wouldn't be in this mess."

"Don't blame Orla, Aunt Fiona," Cat said. "There were many mistakes made, by everyone."

Elinor said, "It seems that you girls have forged a true friendship."

Merida, Cat, and Orla exchanged glances. Cat answered, "We have."

"That's a good thing," Fiona said, "especially for the two of you." She gestured at Merida and Orla. "Since you'll be connected for the rest of your lives."

Elinor sighed. "I suppose we're wasting time talking about blame. What we need to do is plan for the future."

"I agree," Fiona added. "We should make arrangements for the girls' lives together."

Elinor touched Fiona's shoulder. "I promise that our daughters' friendship will continue to grow as Orla is raised at Castle DunBroch."

Fiona's mouth twisted into a frown. "I think you've misunderstood," she said. "There's no way I'll leave my daughter here. But you, Elinor, should feel comfortable in the knowledge that Merida will be well cared for at Cardonagh."

"My daughter is not leaving DunBroch," Elinor declared in her iciest, most queenly voice.

"You are mistaken," Fiona answered, matching Elinor's tone.

Merida had to do something before war was declared between DunBroch and Cardonagh. She and Orla pushed between their mothers to separate them. Merida shouted, "Stop!"

Elinor and Fiona scowled at her instead of each other.

"I need you both to listen to me," Merida said. "What our future will be can only be chosen by Orla and me." She looked directly at Elinor. "I love my family and my homeland, and I cannot imagine leaving it for any reason."

Elinor smiled. "I know, dear."

Merida held up a hand. "But I know Orla

feels the same way about her home and her family." She turned back to Mum and took a deep breath. "I'm very sorry, but I cannot keep my friend from her home. When Lady Fiona's ship returns to Cardonagh, I'll be on board with Orla."

It seemed like everyone in the Great Hall gasped at once. The triplets ran to their sister and clutched at her legs as if they would never let her go. Merida ruffled their hair with her free hand before facing her mother.

The queen's eyes welled up with tears. Merida's own vision began to blur as well, but she had no choice. "I have to do this, Mum," she said.

Elinor reached out and pushed aside a lock of her daughter's tangled hair. She looked into

Merida's eyes. Then she nodded. "I'm proud of you, lass," she said. "This is a great sacrifice to make for your friend."

At that, the tears Merida had been holding back fell freely. Elinor stepped closer and pulled Merida into her arms. "There, there, Daughter," she soothed. "It'll be all right. You're brave and strong, and you can do anything you want."

"But she won't do this," Orla said.

Fiona gasped.

"It's the only way for you to be with your family, Orla," Merida explained.

Orla shook her head. "What kind of a friend would I be if I let you lose your family and your home?" she asked, taking Fiona's hand. "I'm sorry, Mum, but Merida will not be returning to Cardonagh. I will remain here at DunBroch."

It was Fiona's turn to sob. Elinor pulled away from Merida to comfort Fiona. Fergus joined them. Merida took the opportunity to draw Orla aside. "We can't fight about this, Orla. Please let me do this for you. It isn't fair for you to lose your home."

"But I feel the exact same way!" Orla answered. "Taking you from DunBroch is no way for me to treat a friend." She lowered her eyes. "I know we didn't start on the right foot, but I really did want to be your friend. I'm sorry for the way I acted."

Merida sniffed. She didn't want to cry again. "I know I wasn't very friendly when you got here. That was my fault. I was being unfair. I'm sorry, too."

Then there was no more need for words.

Merida threw her arms around Orla and squeezed. Orla hugged her back as hard as she could.

They weren't expecting Cat to scream, "Stop!"

"What's wrong?" Merida asked.

"Look at the two of you!" Cat cried. "Your hands! They're free! The spell is broken!"

Merida and Orla both gaped down at their hands—their unconnected, separate hands.

"Queen Elinor!" Cat shouted. "Aunt Fiona! Look!" She pointed to Merida and Orla.

Elinor and Fiona covered their mouths in shock.

"B-but how?" Fiona stuttered. "How did this happen?"

"I thought the Witch told you binding spells

are unbreakable," Elinor added.

"The binding spell," Merida whispered. "It bound me to Orla." All of a sudden, Merida's head snapped up. She knew what had happened!

She pulled Orla and Cat into another hug. "The spell *is* permanent!" She laughed.

"What?" Orla asked.

Merida grinned. "You and I are bound together for life—bound by friendship."

"All *three* of us are bound by friendship!" Cat added.

"I'm so relieved that the spell is broken," Elinor said, "and I'm glad you've become such good friends. The three of you will be spending hours and hours together right here in this castle. Because you're all *grounded!*"